Dear Avery,
Happy Holidays!
Your friends,
Herbie & Heather Lehman

Herbie & the Smushies

Heather Lehrman

Illustrations by Scott Payne

Acknowledgements

Thanks to my brother Jeremy
for his time, patience and work on this book;
to Steve for all of his support and encouragement;
and most of all to my Boston Terrier Herbie
for being my inspiration!

Herbie is a Boston Terrier who loves to play. Boston Terriers are very friendly dogs with lots of energy. When they are very happy, they make snorting noises like little piggies.

On nice days, Herbie loves to go to the dog park, where he can run, play and make new friends.

Herbie's favorite game is "catch the flying disc." His mommy throws the disc in the air, and Herbie runs after it, jumping high in the air to catch it. He then brings it back to his mommy.

One day, Herbie was having a great time playing when he was surprised by a bigger dog. The bigger dog said, "Give me your toy!"

Herbie said "No, this is my toy! But if you want to play, we can have fun together."

The bigger dog didn't want to play. He wanted to take Herbie's toy and keep it for himself. He pushed Herbie to the ground, leaving him with scratches and bruises. The bigger dog then ran away with Herbie's toy.

Herbie was very upset and wanted to go home. As he was leaving, he noticed a big Bulldog sitting by himself in an empty corner of the dog park. The bulldog was watching Herbie as he left.

At home, Herbie asked his mommy, "Why did that dog knock me down and steal my toy?" Mommy said, "Some dogs are not always going to be nice. That dog was a bully."

"What's a bully?" Herbie asked.

"A bully is a dog who is mean to other dogs for no reason. They pick on other dogs because they look different, are different sizes, are different colors, or even dress differently."

There was a knock at the door. When Mommy opened the door she was surprised to see a big bulldog sitting on her front step.

The bulldog said, "My name is Bruno. I came to visit the little dog who was bullied at the dog park." Bulldogs are medium-sized dogs with massive, short-faced heads. They are gentle, protective, and love children.

Bruno said he was sorry to see what happened at the park. He told Herbie that he was also bullied by the other dogs. "The other dogs say I look ugly because my tongue sticks out and my teeth show. They make fun of me because I breathe heavy." It made Bruno very sad and lonely.

Herbie didn't understand why the other dogs didn't want to play with this very nice bulldog. He asked Bruno if he would like to be friends.

"Yes!" said Bruno, and they became friends.

Herbie was invited to Bruno's house to play. They had a great time running around the backyard.

Herbie noticed that the house across the street from Bruno's was very big and quite nice. "Who lives there?" asked Herbie, pointing at the house.

"That's Lucy and Harley's house. They are French Bulldogs," said Bruno.

"Why don't they come over and play?" asked Herbie.

"I am bigger than they are, and they will think I look mean, like the other dogs do."

"You never know unless you ask," said Herbie.

He then invited them over to play.

The two French Bulldogs were very happy to be asked! French Bulldogs are a breed in the Bulldog family, but are smaller and have big ears that stick up. They are friendly and playful and very happy dogs.

Herbie told them how he and Bruno met.

Harley told the group that he was alone at home for a long time before his Mommy and Daddy decided to get him a friend.

"Then one day they brought my new sister Lucy home, who came from a dog shelter. It took awhile, but she finally grew on me and is my best friend."

"Hey Harley, have you ever been bullied?" asked Bruno.

"Yes, I was on a walk with my Daddy when a big white dog came running over and started a fight with us. All I wanted to do was protect my Daddy, so I had to fight.

It was very scary, but Daddy chased the other dog away. You know dogs are never supposed to be off leash when they are not in their own home or yard."

Lucy then shared her story about being bullied. "Sometimes I go on walks with my Mommy and there is a dog around the block that says mean things about what I wear. My mommy always puts me in fancy collars and warm sweaters, and the dog would always say mean things like,

"Roll out the red carpet, here comes Lucy."

Herbie and Bruno nodded while Lucy continued her story. "I can't help what my mommy buys for me. Our breed gets very cold in the winter so I wear jackets and sweaters. The dog that calls me names has much thicker fur than I do, and doesn't need to wear these things when it's cold. She didn't understand that I need to wear sweaters to keep me warm."

Herbie said, "I like your sweater. I have a sweater too!" The group played together for the rest of the day.

A week or so later, while Herbie was relaxing at home, he heard the sound of a truck outside and ran to the window to see what was going on.

He saw that it was a moving truck. That meant new neighbors were moving in.

Herbie was so excited to see a dog lying on one of the boxes!

"Hi, I'm Jack. I'm a Pug," said the little dog. Pugs are small but sturdy. They are good-natured, playful, and they don't need as much exercise as Boston Terriers like Herbie.

Herbie said, "Wow you look a little like me, with a smushie face! Do you like to play?"

Jack said, "I love to play!"

Herbie told Jack all about his new friends and how they were all bullied in some way by other dogs.

Jack said, "That is terrible. I have been bullied because I am a little guy. I would never bully another dog."

Herbie invited Jack to join his group of friends.

Herbie started having regular play dates with his new group of friends. One day at the dog park, they noticed a little puppy sitting all alone.

"Hi, I'm Herbie, and these are my friends."

"Hi, I am Daisy," said the little dog. "I am a mixed breed: Half French Bulldog and half Boston Terrier." They all greeted Daisy and asked her if she wanted to join them in playing.

Daisy was so happy, that she ran in circles!

Herbie asked Daisy why she was all alone by the entrance to the dog park. Daisy told them "I love to come to the dog park and meet new friends, but I am just a little puppy and sometimes other dogs aren't nice to me."

Daisy thought of the time two large dogs blocked her from entering the park. "These two dogs wouldn't back away from me for a long time, until their owners came and took them away," she said. "I felt so sad, I wanted to cry. It made me afraid to play."

Herbie thought to himself, "Another case of bullying."

A few days later, Herbie was at home playing with his toys when he thought of his new friends: Bruno the Bulldog, Harley and Lucy the French Bulldogs, Jack the Pug, and Daisy the French Bulldog/Boston Terrier puppy.

They all had short snouts and were all called "smush-faced breeds." He was happy that they found each other and were able to share their stories.

Herbie had a thought. "I should form a play group. We won't allow any bullying. Everyone who joins has to be kind and friendly."

Herbie was so excited with his idea. His mommy set up a play date at the park. All of the dogs arrived and Herbie gathered them in a circle. He told them about his idea of a doggie group that welcomed everybody. The gang loved the idea.

"Remember, we were all bullied in some way and it hurt our feelings," Herbie said. "It made us sad and we never want to make any of our new friends sad. As long as the dog is nice and friendly to everybody, they can join our group."

Bruno said, "I never want any dog to be sitting lonely in a corner like I was. If we see someone alone, we will play with them, right?"

"Right," the gang said.

Daisy said, "I would love to greet every new member at the gate of the park and make them feel welcome."

They all agreed. None of them would ever become a bully.

"We should name the group Herbie and the Smushies!" said Jack the Pug.

All the dogs thought this was a great idea. They laughed and played at the dog park for the rest of the day, and every dog they saw was invited to join the Smushies. Herbie couldn't wait to see what kind of adventures they would have together.

The End